Good Evening

A COMEDY-REVUE IN TWO ACTS

By Peter Cook and Dudley Moore

SAMUEL FRENCH, INC.
45 WEST 25TH STREET   NEW YORK 10010
7623 SUNSET BOULEVARD   HOLLYWOOD 90046
LONDON   *TORONTO*

MUSIC—IMPORTANT

Music for this production is available, on a rental and deposit basis in a complete piano vocal score as used in the original Broadway production.

Rental for use of the music is $25.00 for each performance. We can lend you a piano vocal score which was actually used in the New York production, for a period of eight weeks, on receipt of the following:

1. Number of performances and exact performance dates.

2. Rental in full on the music for the entire production.

3. Deposit of $25.00, which is refunded on return to us of the material in good conditions immediately after your production. Plus first-class postage and handling charge of $3.00.

We cannot fill any order for music unless it is accompanied by remittance as above, as all rental material is handled on a strictly c.o.d. basis.

THE PLYMOUTH THEATRE

ALEXANDER H. COHEN and
BERNARD DELFONT

present

PETER DUDLEY
COOK MOORE

in

GOOD EVENING

COMEDY WITH MUSIC

Written by

PETER COOK and DUDLEY MOORE

Directed by   *Designed by*

JERRY ADLER   ROBERT RANDOLPH

PRODUCED IN ASSOCIATION WITH
DONALD LANGDON FOR HEMDALE, LTD.

Good Evening

ACT ONE

HELLO

PETER. Hello.

DUDLEY. Hello.

PETER. How are you?

DUDLEY. I'm terribly well, how are you?

PETER. I'm terribly well as well.

DUDLEY. I must say, you're looking very fit.

PETER. I'm feeling pretty fit actually. Isn't it **amazing**—us just bumping into each other like this?

DUDLEY. Yes, I mean here of all places.

PETER. Here of all places! I mean I haven't seen you since—er—

DUDLEY. Now er hold on a minute—er when was it? Er we, we haven't seen each other . . .

PETER. Well actually we haven't seen each other . . .

DUDLEY. We haven't seen each other . . . er . . . before.

PETER. That's right we've never seen each other before, have we?

DUDLEY. No . . .

PETER. You've never seen me.

DUDLEY. And I've never seen you . . . what a small world.

PETER. What a small world.

DUDLEY. Last thing I expected.

PETER. Well, it must be about a million to one chance.

7

DUDLEY. Oh, more than that.

PETER. Do you think so?

DUDLEY. A couple of billion to one.

PETER. Couple of billion, yes, couple of billion and a half, possibly.

DUDLEY. Yes. Probably three billion to one, the way the world is going.

PETER. Yes, they're breeding like rabbits, aren't they?

DUDLEY. Yes, indeed. Anyway, it's awfully nice to . . . um . . . er . . . see you.

PETER. Well, it's terribly nice to see you.

DUDLEY. Yes. Tell me . . . er . . . are you still doing . . . er . . . whatever you have been doing . . . that is, of course, if you ever do anything.

PETER. Oh, yes. I'm still with the old firm, you know.

DUDLEY. Oh, the old firm.

PETER. Yes, soldiering on— I've just been made a Director in fact.

DUDLEY. Oh, congratulations.

PETER. Well, under somewhat tragic circumstances —er—I've stepped into poor old Bender's shoes. Did you know Bender?

DUDLEY. Bender. The name certainly doesn't ring a bell. Bender who?

PETER. Bender Harrison.

DUDLEY and PETER. (*Together.*) Oh! Bender Harrison—yes.

DUDLEY. No, I've never heard of him.

PETER. You never will now, poor chap. He died last week.

DUDLEY. God! So, poor old Bender's dead.

PETER. Completely dead—yes—yes.

DUDLEY. I'm so sorry. I had no idea.

PETER. Nor did Bender really, he sort of . . . er
. . . keeled over at the office party. Mind you, knowing
Bender the way I knew Bender, which was pretty well,
I think that's the way he would have wanted to go.

DUDLEY. Yes, you knowing Bender the way you must
have known Bender, I'm sure that's the way he must
have wanted to go.

PETER. Yes—yes.

DUDLEY. Not much point lingering on.

PETER. No, he was 106. I tell you the one thing I
really ought to know and that is—how's . . . er . . .
how's your . . . er . . . if you . . . er . . . have a
. . . er.

DUDLEY. My wife? Vera?

PETER. Yeeees. How is she?

DUDLEY. She's awfully well.

PETER. I'm so pleased about that.

DUDLEY. Yes, terribly well, Vera. And of course
young Martin's going to school now.

PETER. Martin going to school. Good God, I had no
idea. How time flies.

DUDLEY. Yes, one moment they're that high—the
next moment, they're . . .

DUDLEY and PETER. (*Together.*) . . . that high.

PETER. Good heavens—Martin at school.

DUDLEY. Yes. Tell me, how's um . . . er . . .
er . . .

PETER. Roger Braintree?

DUDLEY. Yes—how's Roger Braintree?

PETER. Absolutely no idea, I've never met him.
I just saw his name in the telephone book and I er
. . . I was rather hoping you might be able to fill me
in on what Roger's up to.

DUDLEY. I . . . I, . . . I . . . I can't help you there, I'm afraid

PETER. You've no idea what Roger might be doing?

DUDLEY. No . . . well, not apart from what you've told me.

PETER. About him being in the telephone book.

DUDLEY. Yes. Yes—mind you, that's bloody good news.

PETER. Well I'm very pleased for Roger.

DUDLEY. Yes, tremendous— I suppose he is under "B" is he?

PETER. Yes he is, right under "B" which is a . . . pretty bloody good place to start.

DUDLEY. What? . . . B.R.A.I.N.T.R.E.E.?

PETER. The whole thing. Yes . . . he's got his whole thing in there.

DUDLEY. I'm very pleased for Roger.

PETER. Yes, I'm sorry you don't know more about what Roger might be doing in other directions.

DUDLEY. Sorry I can't really help there. Perhaps I could give him a ring this evening and see what he's up to?

PETER. Good idea. Anyway, terribly nice . . . to see you. I . . . I really ought to be dashing back to the office . . . time waits for no man.

DUDLEY. I'd better be toddling along myself, I think.

PETER. Do remember me to . . . er . . . um . . .

DUDLEY. Vera.

PETER. Yes. You must forgive me. I'm terribly bad at names. I keep forgetting them . . .

DUDLEY. Quite all right.

PETER. Do remember me to . . . um . . . er . . .

DUDLEY. Vera.

PETER. That's the chap. And jolly good luck with . . . um . . . er . . . it.

DUDLEY. Yes, well, the same to you—and we must keep in touch.

PETER. Yes, absolutely. I'll give you a tinkle.

DUDLEY. Yes, or vice versa.

PETER. Yes, we must do this again.

DUDLEY. Yes. Goodbye.

PETER. Goodbye. (*They exit.*)

FADE OUT

ON LOCATION

PETER. Good Evening, ladies and gentlemen. You've now seen the entire cast of "GOOD EVENING," and in case you're wondering, which is which, I'm the tall one. For the purpose of the next sketch I'd like you to imagine that Dudley Moore is slightly older than he actually appears on stage. He's playing the part of my father—a man of some seventy-five years of age, and he's just taken these last few seconds to add the necessary ten years. Thank you. (PETER *walks behind door and knocks.*)

DUDLEY. (*Coughs. Opens door.*)

PETER. Hello, Dad.

DUDLEY. Hello, Roger.

PETER. Hello, Dad.

DUDLEY. How's my famous film star son, then, eh?

PETER. I'm fine, Dad, how about you?

DUDLEY. Ah, not so bad, son, 'ere come on in and sit down.

PETER. Oh, thanks, Dad.

DUDLEY. Let's have a look at you—let's have a look

at you—yeh. You're looking a bit more healthy than you did in your last film, I'm glad to say.

PETER. Oh, thanks, Dad.

DUDLEY. Yeh . . . how about a nice cup of tea and a piece of fruit cake?

PETER. Oh, that'd be great, Dad, terrific.

DUDLEY. Right . . . might take a little while . . . (Business *with the tea cart.*)

PETER. That's alright, Dad. (DUDLEY *almost falls over tea trolley.*) You all right Dad?

DUDLEY. Yes, I'm all right. You all right Son? —No bones broken?

PETER. Yes, I'm all right. You all right Dad?

DUDLEY. Okay, Son. . . . (DUDLEY *spills milk.*) Sod it. You don't mind your tea black, do you, son?

PETER. No, I like it continental.

DUDLEY. Continental it will be. Oo, la, la! (DUDLEY *starts to stagger precariously towards* PETER *while carrying two cups of tea.*)

PETER. Can I help you, Dad? You alright?

DUDLEY. Of course, I am. You sit yourself down.

PETER. You okay, Dad? (DUDLEY *gives* PETER *his tea and sits down.*)

DUDLEY. Nothing like a nice cup of tea is there? . . .

PETER. No, Dad, it's great. I feel terrible about not being able to get here earlier.

DUDLEY. Oh, look, son, it's your life. You can't play silly buggers with your career.

PETER. Did Mother understand that, Dad?

DUDLEY. I told her everytime I went to that bloody hospital. I said, Ada, you can't expect a film company to stop a multi-million dollar production in Yugoslavia just because you're feeling a bit under the weather, dear.

PETER. You know, Dad, I tried to get away, but we were shooting this snow sequence and the snow was melting, and the director just refused to release me.

DUDLEY. Of course he refused to release you, Roger, *I* would have refused to release you. Now then. I kept on saying to your Mother, I said, Ada, what is Mr. Omar Sharif going to say if his co-star—our only son —suddenly does a midnight flit out of Yugoslavia just to see his Mother—they'd call him Mummy's Boy, he'd never hear the last of it in the profession.

PETER. So Mother understood the situation did she, Dad?

DUDLEY. Well, I can't vouch for that, son. She went on and on— "Where's my little son, where's my little Roger" —I said—Ada— (*Tea business.* DUDLEY *shakes* PETER'S *arm, spilling his tea.*)

PETER. It's all right, Dad, I've got enough here.

DUDLEY. Try to be a bit more careful.

PETER. Yes. I'm sorry, Dad, I don't know what came over me.

DUDLEY. I said, Ada—he's on location in Yugo— bloody—slavia— I couldn't get through to her.

PETER. It must have been rather tricky for you, Dad.

DUDLEY. She started screaming and hollering, where's my little son, where's my little Roger? In the end they had to move her to a little ward all by herself—well, she was disturbing the transplants—you know, and then she kept on complaining about that— she said, I hate this new ward, I want to go back to the old ward, you know. . . . Stubborn and wilful to the last, your Mother.

PETER. Yes, that's Mum all over.

DUDLEY. Just like with this lovely new house you

bought us—she never really got used to it. Not, of course, to be quite fair, that she had that much time to appreciate it because no sooner had she walked in through that door she started feeling strange and then it was downhill all the way.

PETER. Oh, Dad, you don't think moving to the new house had anything to do with her getting ill, do you?

DUDLEY. (*Gestures indecisively.*) . . . I don't think so, Roger.

PETER. I thought she'd like it here, you know, with the garden and everything like that.

DUDLEY. Oh, it's a lovely garden, Roger, those roses are going to be really nice when I get to them.

PETER. They're lovely roses, Dad, aren't they?

DUDLEY. Oh . . . yes, and don't think I don't appreciate it, son. No. Quite honestly, the thing with your Mother was, she missed some of her old friends, like Mrs. Stringer and Mrs. Booth from one one two . . .

PETER. Yes . . .

DUDLEY. But I'm sure she'd have made new friends, given time, I'm sure I'll make new friends, given time.

PETER. So . . . so you like it here, Dad, do you?

DUDLEY. Ooooh . . . yeeees . . . oh, yes, well, it's much more spacious than Mansfield Road.

PETER. More room for you to sort of dash around in . . .

DUDLEY. Yes. Not, of course, that I need quite so much room now—with your Mother gone . . . (*Sobs,* PETER *taps his head.*) Thank you, Roger. The way I look at it—what you lose on the swings, you gain on the roundabouts . . . Mind you, it's nice having an indoor toilet at my time of life—but your Mother would never go within 2 feet of that indoor toilet.

PETER. I thought she'd like it, Dad.

DUDLEY. I thought she'd revel in it—but you can't

change the habits of a lifetime. Directly we moved
here, she bought a chamber pot and put it down the
bottom of the garden— I think that's how she con-
tracted the pneumonia. Sitting out there on those
frosty nights, the wind howling up her nightie. The
complaints we had about the noise out there—like Guy
Fawkes Night every night.

PETER. I see part of the greenhouse has been broken.

DUDLEY. Yes. She shattered it.

PETER. She what, Dad?

DUDLEY. She shattered it.

PETER. Oh, yes, well, the Delphiniums have come up
nicely.

DUDLEY. Yes, mmm. Everything's come up huge
down there.

PETER. Must be about 12 foot tall.

DUDLEY. Yes, well, your Mother had green fingers
. . . or something like that . . .

PETER. Dad, did you consult that Specialist I told
you about in London?

DUDLEY. No.

PETER. Well, why not, Dad?

DUDLEY. I'll tell you why, son. I didn't want to
offend Dr. Groarke. Now you must understand, Roger,
that Dr. Groarke has always been very good to us.

PETER. I know that, Dad, but . . .

DUDLEY. I mean, he saw you through your German
Measles.

PETER. Yes, Dad, but that was thirty years ago.

DUDLEY. It might have been thirty years ago but
Dr. Groarke has lost none of his acumen. He was
absolutely right about your Mother, you need have no
fears about that, 'cause I asked him, I said, "Dr.
Groarke, you've got to be quite frank with me, what
is the situation concerning my wife, Ada?" He looked

me straight in the eyes—he said, "Norman, your wife is dying, there is no hope" —and he was absolutely spot on. Ada died. Now how can you grumble with that sort of expertise?

PETER. Very accurate diagnosis, wasn't it, Dad?

DUDLEY. Yes. Dr. Groarke is a staggering diagnostician. (DUDLEY *fumbles hopelessly with the word 'diagnostician.'*)

PETER. Dad, is there anything I can do for you at the moment? You know, can I get you anything? Anything you need? Any little luxury?

DUDLEY. Roger, what more could I need? I've got this lovely new house, lovely new colour TV you gave me and your Mother, I couldn't be more comfortable. Oh, Blimey, here's me rattling on—I nearly forgot. Some bits and pieces your Mother set aside she wanted you to have especially. Good job I caught sight of them, she'd never have forgiven me if I'd forgotten. Must get this right—for her sake. (DUDLEY *sorts out "bits and pieces."*) Yes, these first. Here are all your old exercise books and school reports from the County High.

PETER. Oh, thanks, Dad, that will come in handy. Oh, here's an essay I wrote about Spot. (PETER *reads from exercise book.*) "He is a mongrel. We got him from the dog's Home. My Dog is Called Spot."

DUDLEY. (*Reading.*) He was a stray dog and he was starving to death. Someone found him and took him to the Dog's Home where they gave him some dinner and a bath because he had fleas . . . it's a bit boring.

PETER. Not bad for seventeen, Dad.

DUDLEY. And here, here is the illustrated Bible Mum gave you in 1948—you forgot to take it up to town with you when you moved up to your penthouse.

PETER. Sorry, Dad, I forgot it in all the excitement.

DUDLEY. Don't think I don't understand, my boy—I've been young myself, haven't I? And er . . . here is the . . . er . . . aahhh . . . (*Starts to sob.*) I mustn't . . . I mustn't let go . . . Roger, here is your Mother's signet ring she wanted you to have and wear for her. Took me two hours to get it off her bloody finger.

PETER. Well, thanks, Dad, I'll wear it everywhere.

DUDLEY. (*Indicating* PETER'S *finger.*) Just there'll be all right, son. And if you wouldn't mind wearing this black armband in memory of your Mother. I know she'd be pleased because she sewed it especially for you.

PETER. Dad, the one thing I really wanted to know, was, in the end, did Mother die peacefully?

DUDLEY. Roger, your Mother left this life as she lived it, screaming her bloody head off. I remember it very well, it was a Wednesday afternoon, Uncle Ralph had come in for a cup of tea, we hadn't seen him for twenty years and we were, you know, talking about when we used to walk over the cliffs at Leigh on Sea watching the boats come in—he's a boring bugger, that Ralph—once every twenty years is good enough for me.

PETER. Yes, Dad.

DUDLEY. Anyway, Mother was lying very quietly, very still, almost at rest and suddenly, without a word of a lie, she sat bolt upright in bed, she went, "Aargh" (*Screams.*) her false teeth hit the ceiling and that was it.

PETER. Oh, Dad, I just wish I could have been there.

DUDLEY. Your Mother never did anything by halves —both sets—POW—hit the electric light bulb, the bulb fell to the floor, smashed, matron came running in, slipped on the broken glass, hit her head on the bedpost, killed outright . . . Nurse Oviatt, hearing the commotion, came roaring in from the President Roosevelt Memorial Ward, tripped over matron and went flying out the window. She fell five stories onto a car that was coming into the forecourt. It was an open car, she killed herself and the two passengers. The weight of the three dead bodies on the accelerator took that car roaring into the catering department, killed seven nurses, knocked ten orderlies into a huge vat of boiling potatoes. Well naturally, the valve on the vat got stuck and there was a tremendous explosion— and the first floor collapsed. Well you can imagine what that did to the second and third floors. Anyway, son, I won't bore you with details—suffice it to say, that I was the sole survivor. Nine hundred and eighty-seven people wiped out in a flash of your Mother's teeth.

PETER. Oh, Dad. I just feel so guilty that I couldn't have been there.

DUDLEY. There's nothing for you to feel guilty about: there's nothing anybody human could have done. You were on location, Roger. You were on location.

PETER. Dad, I really ought to be getting back to London. I've got this meeting.

DUDLEY. Of course you have, Roger.

PETER. Mr. Broccolli has just got back from Brussels and I've got this rather important meeting with Cubby.

DUDLEY. I'm sorry to keep you hanging about like this, Roger.

Ding-a-ding-a ding, Ding-a-ding-a ding,
Ding-a-ding-a ding, ding ding ding ding-a-dong,
With a fa, la, la, and a ding-a ding ding,
Jug, jug, pee-wee, twit-a-woo fa,
La, la, la, la, la, la.

FADE OUT

CRIME AND PUNISHMENT

(DUDLEY *in schoolmaster outfit paces room. There is
a KNOCK on door.*)

DUDLEY. Come in.

PETER. You sent for me, sir?

DUDLEY. Yes, I did indeed, Rawlings. (*Clears his
throat.*) Rawlings, I had a rather distressing piece of
news this morning. As you know, three generations of
Rawlings have brought distinction and credit to this
school.

PETER. Yes, sir.

DUDLEY. Your father, your grandfather and your
great-grandfather have all, in their time, been head
boy of the school.

PETER. Yes, sir.

DUDLEY. You, yourself, are in line for this privilege
when Whitwell leaves the school next year and goes up
to Oxford to study forestry. However, Rawlings, I was
rather disappointed to hear from Mr. Asprey, the
physical training master, that a pair of very valuable
gymnasium slippers disappeared from his stock room
Tuesday last and reappeared as if by magic in your
locker next to a copy of *Busty Beauties Around the
World.*

PETER. Yes, sir.

DUDLEY. Well, do you have any explanation for the appearance of these gym shoes in your locker, other than the one that immediately springs to mind?

PETER. No, sir. I wanted the gym shoes, sir, and I took them.

DUDLEY. You wanted the gym shoes, Rawlings, and you took them?

PETER. Yes, sir.

DUDLEY. Good God, man, do you realize what would happen in this world if people took exactly what they wanted?

PETER. Sir . . .

DUDLEY. We'd be living in a sea of anarchy, the whole moral fibre of society would fall apart! You feel you're somebody unique and exempt from these basic laws of human behavior?

PETER. No, sir.

DUDLEY. Do you feel that the ethics of a civilized society should apply to everyone except yourself?

PETER. No, sir.

DUDLEY. Are you some latter-day Hitler, Rawlings, who feels he can annex whatever he wants? Today gym shoes, tomorrow the world! It is my responsibility, Rawlings, to douse the flames of such over-weening ambition, to exorcise this creeping cancer. And you will find, Rawlings, not for me the policy of appeasement. Oh, no! Like Churchill, I will fight you on the beaches, I will fight you in the air, I will repell your doodle bugs, I will snatch your Messerschmidts from the sky! You may gather, Rawlings, there is only one course open to me. I must punish you very severely. I must ask you to bend over this desk and take six of the best.

PETER. Yes, sir. Could I just say one thing, sir?

DUDLEY. Well, come on, Rawlings, out with it. But I'm afraid you'll find that any plea for mercy will fall on deaf ears.

PETER. I did take the slippers, sir, and I deserve to be punished, and you're much older and wiser than I am, sir . . .

DUDLEY. Come on, Rawlings, out with it!

PETER. I'm much bigger than you are, sir, and if you lay a finger on me I'll smash your stupid little face in.

DUDLEY. (*Pause.*) Rawlings, why didn't you tell me all this before?

PETER. Sorry, sir.

DUDLEY. Well, Rawlings, this puts a completely different complexion on the whole thing! Now, Rawlings, I'd like you to accept on behalf of the school, my private collection of *Screw* Magazine, this excellent deck of Acapulco Gold, here's ten pounds, why don't you pop up to the school nurse, present her my compliments and have her give you a deep, relaxing Swedish massage on me . . .

FADE OUT

DUDLEY MOORE

DIE FLABBERGAST

Ich meine Hunste far die Flabbergast
Und Swein-Hunds divein hein Heinst.
Mein is eine veine, is meine,
Mein is eine veine, is meine,
Mein is eine—Ah! (*Screech.*)

Ich meine swein, ach is mein is mein is mein is
    mein is mein—Ach!
Mein is a veine, mein is a vein,
Mein is a veine, mein is a vein,
Ich mein ich vein, mein is a vein,
Ich mein ich mit ein mit ein,
Mit ein mit ein mit ein mit ein
Mit ein mit ein mit—Ah—Aaar (*Growl.*)!

(*NOTE: The song is sung by one voice, alternating
between tenor and soprano range, as in a duet.
The words are mainly gibberish, and may be
altered to suit the convenience of the singer, who
may find certain sounds easier to sing than others.
The only words that should be unchanged are "Die
Flabbergast."*)

FADE OUT

DOWN THE MINE

JUDGE. Yes I could have been a judge but I didn't
have the Latin. I never had sufficient Latin for the
judging exams; they're very rigorous the judging
exams, they're noted for their rigour; people come
staggering out of the judging exams shouting "Oh my
God, what a rigorous exam"; so I became a minor in-
stead, a coal miner; I managed to get through the
mining exams; they're not very rigorous; they only ask
you one question; they say "Who are you?" and I
got 75% on that. But the trouble is that all the people
down the mine are not as intelligent as I am . . .
I'm not saying you get a load of riffraff down the
mimes. I'm just saying we've got a load of riffraff down
my mine; they're very boring conversationalists; all
they talk about is what goes on in the mine which

isn't very much; if ever you want to hear a conversation like "Hello, I've just found a lump of coal; have you really? Yes there's no doubt about it, this black substance is coal alright; jolly good, the very thing we're looking for." If you want to hear a conversation like that, then just pop down my mine . . . it goes on all the time. I've often tried to make the conversation a bit more stimulating. I once said to one of my colleagues "have you heard of Marcel Proust?" and he said, "No. I think he must work in some other mine." So I explained that Mr. Proust was a writer who dipped biscuits into his tea and whenever he did that all his past memories came flooding back. So this other fellow said, "Why don't I try that" so he dipped a biscuit in his tea and sure enough all his memories came flooding back . . . a strange look came over his face and he said, "All my memories are flooding back; I can remember coming down the mine one day and I saw a lump of coal and I picked it up and put it on a trolley" and I said, "Is that all you can remember?" and he said, "Yes." It's not enough to keep the mind alive, is it? It must be nice to be a famous writer like Marcel Proust, drinking tea and writing down all you remember . . . then you get into your white sports car and drive along the street shouting out to ladies "Hello lovely lady, I'm a very famous writer, jump into my speedy roadster and I'll take you back to my place and immortalize you." That's why I do a bit of writing on the side. I've written a book about my experiences down the mine. I've called it "My experiences down the Mine" in order to give the public an indication of what the plot is all 'bout. It's about a man who goes down the mine one day and sees a lump of coal quite near him, so he grabs the lump of coal and puts it on a trolley and the trolley wheels down a long dark tunnel and he never sees it again. That's the story. I think it's a comment on the meaninglessness of life; it's a very short story but it's also extremely boring. I fell asleep the first time I read it through. I took it along to a publisher and he confirmed my opinion; he said it was probably the most boring story he had ever read; and he's not a man who's given to superlatives. He said, "The main trouble with your story is that it lacks everything. You name it, it lacks it, and above all" he said, "it lacks the elements of sex and violence which are so vital to us in these troubled times"; of course he was quite right so I've spiced it up a bit. I've kept to the main story outline but I've changed the title to "Sex and Violence Down the Mine." It's about these three naked women, Beryl, Stella, and Margaret, who are very sexy and violent; and they are wandering about the desert kicking each other in the stomach looking for kicks; they wander along for several days kicking each other; it's very sexy and violent; then, suddenly, Beryl Whittington, who is the leader of the nude women kicks Stella in the teeth and says, "Hello, isn't that a mine shaft over there? . . . why don't we all go down it and do provocative things to each other." So, as one man, the three girls rush down the mine and start throwing lumps of coal at each other in an amazingly sexy and violent way. Quite soon they are all exhausted and completely covered in coal dust, so they lie down and go to sleep. And now comes the interesting twist. A miner, whose character is very closely based on mine, stumbles across the three sleeping bodies, but as they are completely covered in coal dust he mistakes them for lumps of coal. "Aha" he says, "three lumps of coal," and he picks them up and throws them on a trolley that disappears down a long dark tunnel and he never sees

them again. It's a very sad story and it's also very
moral. It tries to make the point that if you spend
your whole life wandering around in the nude kicking
each other and doing sexy things you'll end up as
a lump of coal. I think Proust would have been proud
of it. Whoops! Did you notice for no apparent reason I
suddenly went "Whoops"? It's an impediment I picked
up from being down the mine. Whoops! 'Cause one
day I was walking along in the dark— Whoops!
—and I saw the body of a dead pit pony Whoops!
I went in surprise and ever since then I've been going
"whoops!" unexpectedly and that's another reason
why I couldn't have been a judge. It would destroy
the dignity of the Court. One day I might have been
up there sentencing away, all dignified and regal in
my robes, and I'd have been sentencing the criminal
and saying "You have been found guilty of murder
and I sentence you to "Whoops!" " and you see under
the English law, that would have to stand. But all in
all, I would much rather have been a judge than a
coal miner, because being a miner as soon as you get
too old and tired and sick and stupid to do the job
properly, you have to go. Well, the very opposite ap-
plies to the judges. It's a pity, really, because I've always been after the trappings of great luxury. I really
have. And yet all I've got hold of is the trappings of
great poverty. I've got hold of the wrong load of trappings and a rotten load of trappings they are.

FADE OUT

ONE LEG TOO FEW

PETER. Miss Rigby! Stella, my love! Would you send
in the next auditioner, please. (*Enter* DUDLEY *hopping*

on one leg. The other is held up by his free hand and concealed under a coat.) Mr. Spiggott, I believe it is.

DUDLEY. Yes—Spiggott's the name, acting's the game. (DUDLEY *follows* PETER *around stage, taps him on shoulder and hops away.*) You're it!

PETER. We're not here to play tag, Mr. Spiggott. Now, if you'll settle down for one moment, please. Now, Mr. Spiggott, you are, are you not, auditioning for the role of Tarzan.

DUDLEY. Right.

PETER. Now, Mr. Spiggott, I couldn't help noticing almost immediately that you are a one-legged man.

DUDLEY. You noticed that?

PETER. I noticed that, Mr. Spiggott. When you have been in the business as long as I have, you get to notice these little things almost instinctively. Now, Mr. Spiggott, you, a one-legged man, are applying for the role of Tarzan—a role traditionally associated with a two-legged artiste.

DUDLEY. Correct.

PETER. And yet, you a unidexter, are applying for the role.

DUDLEY. Right.

PETER. A role for which two legs would seem to be the minimum requirement.

DUDLEY. True.

PETER. Well, Mr. Spiggott, need I point out to you with overmuch emphasis where your deficiency lies as regards landing the role?

DUDLEY. Yes, I think you ought to.

PETER. Need I say with too much stress that it is in the leg division that you are deficient.

DUDLEY. The leg division?

PETER. Yes, the leg division, Mr. Spiggott. You are deficient in the leg division. To the tune of one. Your right leg I like. It's a lovely leg for the role. As soon as I saw it come in. I said, "Hullo. What a lovely leg for the role." I've got nothing against your right leg. The trouble is—neither have you. You fall down on your left.

DUDLEY. You mean it's inadequate?

PETER. Yes, it's inadequate, Mr. Spiggott. And to my mind, the public is just not ready for the sight of a one-legged Tarzan swinging through the jungly tendrils, shouting "Hello, Jane!"

DUDLEY. Oh.

PETER. However, don't despair, Mr. Spiggott. After all, you score over a man with no legs at all.

DUDLEY. Well, I've got twice as many. So there's still hope?

PETER. Of course, there is still hope. If we get no two-legged character actors in here within the next 18 months, there is every chance that you, a unidexter, will be the very sort of person we shall be attempting to contact.

DUDLEY. Oh, thank you. (*Shakes* PETER's *hand and hops up and down.*)

PETER. Sorry I can't be more definite, but you must understand with the state of the industry today, we can't afford to take any risks whatever . . . (DUDLEY *hops off.*)

FADE OUT

SOAP OPERA

(*The doorbell rings.* PETER *goes and opens it.* DUDLEY *is there, dressed in jeans and a T-shirt.*)

DUDLEY. Hello, blue eyes. (*Enters swishily and sings.*) "There's no Business Like Show Business . . ."

PETER. Excuse me. What can I do for you?

DUDLEY. It's more of a question of what I can do for you, isn't it, love? I'm your new daily, your new Mrs. Mop.

PETER. You're the temporary domestic?

DUDLEY. Yeeeees.

PETER. I . . . I'm sorry, I was expecting the agency to send me a woman.

DUDLEY. (*Laughs.*) Well, you'll have to make do with me then, won't you? Oh, I love your place, I think it's absolutely super.

PETER. Oh, thank you very much.

DUDLEY. You a bachelor?

PETER. Yes, bachelor gay, that's me.

DUDLEY. Me too . . . mm . . . You may have guessed, this isn't my normal sort of work.

PETER. Well, I did get an inkling when you came in through the door.

DUDLEY. No, I'm an actor, actually.

PETER. Oh, an actor.

DUDLEY. Yes. I'm resting between engagements, you know—mind you, not that I don't like this sort of work—I absolutely adore it—because one gets to meet all sorts of interesting people, and I was terribly excited when I was assigned to you, because do you know, I've never met a barrister before. (*Sits on sofa.*)

PETER. Would you mind not sitting on my briefs?

DUDLEY. (*Picks up ribbon.*) —What's this, dear?

PETER. It's the little pink ribbon I tie round my briefs.

DUDLEY. Oh, well, that's our little secret. I suppose being a barrister is rather like being an actor, isn't it?

PETER. I don't really see the connection, no.

DUDLEY. Well. You call it "acting for your client," don't you?

PETER. In rather a different way.

DUDLEY. Course you do . . . dragging up in all those lovely cozies and wigs swishing round the Courtroom, appealing to the Jury . . . ooooh . . . gentlemen of the jury, I put it to you . . . My client has a foolproof alibi . . . on the night of the twentieth . . .

PETER. I can assure you it's nothing like that in Court.

DUDLEY. I bet it is . . . I once played a Q.C. in an Agatha Christie play in Croydon. They used to call me A.C.-Q.C. backstage—you get a lot of giggles in the profession.

PETER. Yes . . . the washing up is just through there. (*Points to kitchen.*)

DUDLEY. Oh, bonky-bonk, down to earth again— wretch. Have you got any rubber gloves, dear?

PETER. Yes, Mrs. Higgins keeps them by the sink.

DUDLEY. It's because I have a very sensitive skin, you know. I've only got to touch a flake of detergent and woosh, I get a terrible rash all over my body, and as an actor, you know, one can't afford that sort of thing in these days of full frontal. Gesture, expression, projection—one can't do that with a spotty botty! (*Laughs. Picks up some record albums.*) Ooooh . . . I see you like Opera.

PETER. Yes, I do enjoy Opera. Why?

DUDLEY. (*Looking at the albums.*) Oh . . . Bona . . . Bona . . .

PETER. I don't know that one. Is that a new one?

DUDLEY. Silly. (*He picks out a record.*) Oooh, Lucia di Lammermoor—one of my favorites. I love that bit where she comes out singing in her nightdress, and she sings that beautiful bit, remember? (*He sings from "Lucia".*) I bet your Mrs. Higgins doesn't do that for you.

PETER. No, but she does do quite a **lot of** washing up.

DUDLEY. Oh, touché. Well, sleeves up, gloves on, I'm the boy for liquid Joy. (*He exits. Phone rings.* PETER *answers it.*)

PETER. Hello . . . what? . . . oh . . . I see . . . hold on. (*Shouts to kitchen.*) It's for you.

DUDLEY. (*Enters.*) Who is it, love?

PETER. It's some woman.

DUDLEY. Oh, wrong number, dear. (*Exits.*)

PETER. (*To phone.*) Hello . . . it sounds very much like him. (*Shouts to kitchen.*) She insists it's for you.

DUDLEY. (*Enters.*) Ooooh . . .

PETER. (*To phone.*) He's just coming.

DUDLEY. Mmmmmm . . . thank you so much . . . (*Takes phone very cautiously.*) Hello, who is this? Oh Gloria. I thought I was getting kinky phone calls. (*Aside to* PETER.) It's my agent, the only woman in my life.

PETER. Well, she shouldn't be ringing you here.

DUDLEY. I quite agree. (*To phone.*) Gloria, we must be brief, otherwise I'll have the law on me. (*To* PETER.) Hope springs eternal. (*To phone.*) You're joking . . . fantastico-issimay . . . do I know the scene, dear? I've been rehearsing it for the last six weeks. When's the audition? Tomorrow morning, love—oh, I can't possibly . . . All right, all right love, I'll be there on the dot. Thank you so much. God bless you—good-bye, heart . . . mmmm . . . (*Blows kiss to phone. Hangs up.*)

PETER. What on earth was that all about?

DUDLEY. Oh, must sit down. I'm up for Othello. Oh, I say, you wouldn't do me a special favor, would you?

PETER. I very much doubt it.

DUDLEY. No, I mean you wouldn't just give me five

minutes of your time and go through my lines with
me, would you, cos I've got my audition tomorrow
morning.

PETER. What about the washing up—you've hardly
started on that?

DUDLEY. I'll work my fingers to the bone if you'll
just give me five minutes of your time.

PETER. Just read through a few lines, that's all, then
you promise to do some work.

DUDLEY. Cross my legs and hope to die. Have you
got a copy of "Othello?"

PETER. Yes, I've got one somewhere.

DUDLEY. Oh, you are a brick.

PETER. Just a few lines. (PETER *gets book from
shelf.*)

DUDLEY. Could we do Act Five, Scene Two? (DUD-
LEY *looks at* PETER's *book.*) Oh, you've got the same
edition.

PETER. Yes, I rather go for Penguins.

DUDLEY. Mmm—each to his own, dear. Act Five,
Scene Two is where Desdemona has dropped her hanky
and Iago has been whispering all those awful things
in Othello's ear.

PETER. Yes, I know the scene . . . yes.

DUDLEY. A scene of tremendous jealousy. (*Out to
audience.*) Oh, I know in my bones that I'm going to
become Othello. (*To* PETER.) When I play a part,
love, I really am that part.

PETER. I can't promise to do the same for Desdemona.

DUDLEY. You'll be lovely. 'Ere—why don't you wear
your wig? It'll make you feel the part . . . (PETER
puts on his barrister's wig.) Ooooh, you drag up beauti-
fully.

DUDLEY. Line sixty-three. Good Luck. Merde. (*Reads.*)

BY HEAVENS I SAW MY HANDERCHIEF
    IN'S HANDS

O PERJURED WOMAN. THOU DOST STONE
    MY HEART

AND MAK'ST ME CALL WHAT I INTEND
    TO DO

A MURDER, WHICH I THOUGHT A
    SACRIFICE.

I SAW THE HANDKERCHIEF.

    PETER. (*Without any passion.*)

HE FOUND IT THEN

I NEVER GAVE IT HIM

SEND FOR HIM HITHER

LET HIM CONFESS THE TRUTH.

    DUDLEY. Oh, a bit more life, dear. A bit more vigor.

    PETER. Oh, I see. You want something to bounce off, do you?

    DUDLEY.

HE HATH CONFESSED

    PETER. (*Very passionately.*)

WHAT, MY LORD?

    DUDLEY.

Ooooooh.

THAT HE HATH USED THEE.

    PETER.

HOW? UNLAWFULLY?

    DUDLEY.

AYE.

(*Bangs hand hard on door.*)

Ooooh, Bugger.

    PETER. I don't have that in my text.

    DUDLEY. What, dear?

PETER. I don't have a "Bugger" in my Penguin.

DUDLEY. (*Annoyed.*) I'll give you a bugger in your Penguin mate.

PETER. Could we get on—I'm just feeling the part of Desdemona.

DUDLEY. Where were we, love?

PETER. Line seventy-one.

DUDLEY. (*Sing-song.*) Oh, seventy-one, never been done, Queen of all the Fairies.

PETER.

HE WILL NOT SAY SO.

DUDLEY.

NO, HIS MOUTH IS STOPPED.

HONEST IAGO HATH TAKEN ORDER FOR'T.

PETER.

O, MY FEAR INTERPRETS. WHAT IS HE DEAD?

DUDLEY.

HAD ALL HIS HAIRS BEEN LIVES,

MY GREAT REVENGE HAD STOMACH FOR THEM ALL.

PETER.

ALAS, HE IS BETRAYED, AND I UNDONE.

DUDLEY.

OUT, STRUMPET. WEEP'ST THOU FOR HIM TO MY FACE?

PETER.

OH BANISH ME, MY LORD, BUT KILL ME NOT.

(*Grabs* DUDLEY *by the shirt and pulls him.*)

DUDLEY. Blimey, you didn't half give my left nipple a going over. It's gone all perky.

DOWN, STRUMPET.

PETER.

KILL ME TOMORROW: LET ME LIVE
   TONIGHT

(*Grabs him again.*)

DUDLEY. Not the other one. Oooh, I'm all aglow.

NAY IF YOU STRIVE—

PETER.

BUT HALF AN HOUR

(*Grabs* DUDLEY *again.*)

DUDLEY.

Here!

BEING DONE

THERE IS NO PAUSE

PETER.

BUT WHILE I SAY ONE PRAYER

DUDLEY.

IT IS TOO LATE

(*He grabs* PETER *by the throat and chokes him.*)

PETER. Oh, Lord!

DUDLEY. (*Has* PETER *down on the couch and chokes him until all is still.*) Bloody fabulous. You've acted before, haven't you? (PETER *is quite still, obviously dead.*) Oh, my God. I went over the top again. (*Pause.*) Ooooh . . . now I can have my first go at mouth to mouth resuscitation. (*He bends over* PETER, *pauses. Sees audience observing, shouts to wings.*) . . . Ere! . . . curtain . . . curtain. (*He bends over* PETER *again as the curtain falls.*)

FADE OUT

ACT TWO

GOSPEL TRUTH

(PETER, *dressed as a Shepherd, is seated. We hear sounds of sheep in the background.*)

PETER. Stop that, get off her . . . she's only young . . . and you . . . get off . . . (DUDLEY *enters, dressed in robes and carrying a scroll and quill pen.*)

DUDLEY. I believe you are Mr. Arthur Shepherd.

PETER. That's right, Shepherd by name and shepherd by nature. Lo my flock a-lowing.

DUDLEY. (*Pleased at his joke.*) 'ello . . . 'ello . . .

PETER. That's jolly good that, I never thought of that.

DUDLEY. Yeh, it's a new one on me.

PETER. (*Looking at sheep.*) That's a new one on 'er . . . will you get off, stop that . . . get off.

DUDLEY. Let me introduce myself.

PETER. Yes.

DUDLEY. My name is Matthew.

PETER. 'ello, Matthew.

DUDLEY. 'ello, Arthur—you may have heard of me and my colleagues Mark, Luke and John? . . .

PETER. Oh, yeh . . . yeh . . . I've heard of you lot —you're celebrities. Can I touch your raiment?

DUDLEY. Certainly.

PETER. (*He touches* DUDLEY's *robe.*) Knockout.

DUDLEY. Yes, well, er . . . we are doing an in-depth profile of Jesus, or the Messiah as you may know him.

PETER. No, I don't.

DUDLEY. You don't know him?

PETER. Well, yes, I do—I know him as Jesus.

DUDLEY. Oh fine . . .

PETER. Not that other thing. Which paper do you work for?

DUDLEY. The Bethlehem Star.

PETER. Oh, yeh . . . the wife and I take the Star actually.

DUDLEY. Oh?

PETER. I don't think much of your Racing Correspondent.

DUDLEY. Oh?

PETER. I had three shekels on that camel in the 3.15 at Galilee—it's still bloody running, that one is . . .

DUDLEY. I don't work on that side of the paper— I work on the more serious side, you know, rapportage . . . and . . . we're doing this in-depth profile of Jesus, and I gather that you were actually in on the very first moments surrounding the birth of the Holy Child.

PETER. Yes . . . I was . . . yeh . . .

DUDLEY. That is marvellous . . . now what I'd like you to do, if you are willing, is to tell me what happened, in your own words.

PETER. Yes. Well it's quite simple, really . . . er . . . basically what happened was that me and the lads were abiding in the fields.

DUDLEY. (*Writing.*) Abiding in the fields . . . yes . . .

PETER. Yes . . . mind you, I can't abide these fields . . .

DUDLEY. No?

PETER. I mean, look around you—they are unabidable fields.

DUDLEY. Yeh . . .

PETER. I'd say these are about the most unabidable bleeding fields I've ever had to abide in.

DUDLEY. Yeh . . . I'll abide by that. (DUDLEY *laughs at his joke.* PETER *is unmoved.*) No . . . no . . . my apologies, Arthur. You were abiding in the fields? . . .

PETER. . . . and we were watching our flocks by night.

DUDLEY. (*Writing.*) Watching our flocks by night . . . yeh . . .

PETER. Yes . . . cos that's when you have to watch 'em, you know, that's when they get up to all their rubbish.

DUDLEY. Yeh . . . yeh . . .

PETER. Hot Summer nights, the rams go mad— (*He points.*) specially that one over there, he's a dirty little bugger (*He shouts.*) —cut that out . . . (*To* DUDLEY.) doing it in broad daylight, in front of you, a Holy Man . . .

DUDLEY. Ah . . . it's only Human.

PETER. Yeh, I may be a bit old-fashioned, but I don't like to see one ram doing it to another.

DUDLEY. (*Looking intently at sheep.*) Oh, yes . . . he's an enthusiast, isn't he?

PETER. Oh, yeh—top marks for enthusiasm, zero for accuracy.

DUDLEY. It's a bit distracting, isn't it?

PETER. Yeh, sorry about all those ramifications going on down there though—I've got no control over them . . .

DUDLEY. Oh, they're only young once.

PETER. Yeah, I think I'll get my next lot from Gommorah.

DUDLEY. (*Turning back to* PETER.) Anyway . . . you were abiding in the fields, watching your flocks by night . . .

PETER. Yeah . . .

DUDLEY. And then what happened?

PETER. Well . . . er . . . much to our surprise, the Angel of the Lord flew down.

DUDLEY. Oh . . . now that must have been a fantastic experience.

PETER. Well, it made a break, you know . . . bit of a break just from abiding, him flashing down like that.

DUDLEY. Tell me, Arthur, how did you know it was the Angel of the Lord?

PETER. Oh, I'll tell you what the giveaway was, Matthew. It was this ethereal glow he was emanating . . . he was emanating an ethereal glow.

DUDLEY. Oh, oh, I see.

PETER. And as soon as I saw Him emanating I said 'ello—Angel of the Lord.

DUDLEY. Halo?

PETER. Uh, halo, certainly, yes. Halo and goodbye we said afterwards. He wasn't there for long, he just gave his little message, and then He was off like a bat out of 'ell.

DUDLEY. Yeh . . . wings?

PETER. Oh . . . wings . . . Matthew . . . I've never seen such a gorgeous pair on a man before.

DUDLEY. Yeh?

PETER. They were outstanding wings, all gossamer, shimmering there in the starlight.

DUDLEY. Oh, it must have been remarkable.

PETER. Yes, it was, I noticed it.

DUDLEY. What did He say to you, Arthur?

PETER. Well, he . . . . he . . . he sort of singled me out from the other lowly shepherd folk—

DUDLEY. Oh, lovely . . .

PETER. . . . and He said, "Unto ye a Child is born. Unto ye a Son is given."

DUDLEY. Yes. What was your reaction?

PETER. Total shock. I mean, I wasn't even married at the time and I thought, you know, Blimey what was I doin' this time last year? . . .

DUDLEY. Yeah . . .

PETER. . . . could it be that little bird I met down the Shepherd's Delight? . . .

DUDLEY. Yeah . . .

PETER. . . . but the Angel of the Lord went on to explain that when He said "ye," he didn't mean me personal like, he meant "ye" in the sense of the whole world. Unto the whole world a Child is born . . . unto the whole world a Son is given.

DUDLEY. Yes. He was using the universal 'ye.'

PETER. Was he? Well I wouldn't know, I'm not educated myself.

DUDLEY. Yes. Yes, that's what He was using. The universal ye.

PETER. Good for him. And He went on to say, "Ye shall find the Child lying in a manger—all meanly wrapped in swaddling clothes."

DUDLEY. Oh, lovely language . . .

PETER. Yes, He was very effluent.

DUDLEY. Yes. I suppose your first reaction was to whip over there and have a peep, eh?

PETER. Well, naturally we all dashed down to the stable, but when I arrived I was in for a bit of a shock.

DUDLEY. Really? Go on.

PETER. I will. Cos when He said "ye shall find the Child all meanly wrapped in swaddling clothes," I thought to myself, fair enough, He'll be fairly meanly wrapped. Nothing flashy, nothing gaudy.

DUDLEY. Yes.

PETER. But when I arrived, it was diabolical. It was the meanest bit of wrapping I've ever seen—what's more, that kid was barely swaddled. I'd say, it was the worst job of wrapping and swaddling I have ever seen in my life.

DUDLEY. How very distressing.

PETER. It was alarming to behold.

DUDLEY. Now, Arthur, I want you to think back in time . . .

PETER. Well, I'll do it now, if you like.

DUDLEY. No, what I meant was, think back now— to then.

PETER. That's what I meant—think back to then, now.

DUDLEY. Right. Now then—what was the atmosphere like in the stable on this joyous, historic occasion?

PETER. The atmosphere in the stable was very, very smelly—with all these cows and goats and sheep about, you know. And they had no sense of occasion . . .

DUDLEY. That's a fascinating sidelight, but what I'm really after, Arthur is—what was the atmosphere like amongst the . . . members of the Holy family?

PETER. Oh, I see, the personal atmosphere—

DUDLEY. Yes.

PETER. Well, in one word—tense.

DUDLEY. Tense? You surprise me.

PETER. Joseph in particular. He was sitting in the corner of the stable looking very gloomy indeed.

DUDLEY. Well he might have been feeling a bit disgruntled not being the real father.

PETER. I think that was it. I think he felt left out of the whole thing, you know—and, er . . . personally, I think this is why he done such a rotten job on the swaddling—he just couldn't be bothered to swaddle. . . . And let's face it, there had been a lot of tittle-tattle about his wife and the 'oly Ghost. I mean, rumors had been flying round Bethlehem—as indeed the 'oly Ghost must have been.

DUDLEY. Was the Holy Ghost there?

PETER. Hard to say. He's an elusive little bugger at the best of times—and I did not see Him. I was very disappointed because I felt strongly at the time He should have been there. You know, in His capacity as the Godfather.

DUDLEY. Especially after His treatment of the Virgin Mary—making Her an offer She couldn't refuse.

PETER. Well, making Her an offer She didn't even notice.

DUDLEY. I gather that later on in the evening the three wise men came by. Am I right?

PETER. Yeh, three wise men arrived, yeh—three bloody idiots if ever I saw any. In they come, called themselves Magi. (*Pronounced "Maggie."*)

DUDLEY. Three blokes came in and called themselves Magi?

PETER. Yeah. They peered around the stable door and said, "Hello, we're Magi."

DUDLEY. How very embarrassing.

PETER. We didn't know where to look—and they were bearing these gifts—gold, frankincense and myrrh.

DUDLEY. (*Trying to spell it.*) That's M-"ER"-H. Nice of them to bring these gifts, eh?

PETER. Well—I suppose the gold was welcome, but what's a little kid going to do wth frankincense and myrrh, I ask you?

DUDLEY. Right.

PETER. I mean, myrrh's that stuff what poofs put behind their ears, isn't it?

DUDLEY. Yes.

PETER. That over-perfumed jelly stuff, but *Jesus*, He was so polite about it. He sat up in the manger, He adjusted His swaddling and He said "Thank you, gentlemen, for these lovely prezzies, I hope you have a safe trip back—Merry Christmas."

FADE OUT. The following material is optional.

DUDLEY. Little love.

PETER. A little charmer.

DUDLEY. Precocious, eh?

PETER. Yes, well, talking at half an hour old, it's good going, isn't it? Tell me, when He did become a man, He never got married, did He?

DUDLEY. No, no. Like Father, like Son.

PETER. I see. In that case, who looked after Him. I mean, who did the little things about the house, like the washing up, His undies, you know, little things like that?

DUDLEY. He had a lovely landlady, a certain Mrs. McMeier.

PETER. McMeier?

DUDLEY. Yes . . . lovely old girl, and Mark, one of my colleagues, was lucky enough to track her down and have a few words with her.

(PETER *and* DUDLEY *take on two other characters for an interview.*)

MARK. (PETER.) Mrs. McMeier, I understand that you actually knew Jesus.

MRS. McMEIER. (DUDLEY, *in drag*.) Yes, thank you and hello. Mr. Jesus was in residence at Dead Sea View for many happy years—er—he was a model lodger, you know, very well behaved, he didn't have girls in his room or anything smutty like that.

MARK. I believe also that you did the cooking for him.

MRS. McMEIER. Oh, yes. I used to do him a packed lunch, every day, mostly low calorie stuff, you know— unleavened bread, goat's cheese and that sort of thing, because he used to like to keep himself in trim. He used to say to me, "Mrs. McMeier, if I'm going to save the world I've got to keep myself in trim, not go to seed like that great, fat Buddha."

MARK. Did he ever have any problems at all with his health?

MRS. McMEIER. No, not at all, no, he was a very healthy man. I do remember one time, however, he came back from an afternoon out with his feet absolutely sopping wet—I said, "Mr. Jesus, where on earth have you been"—he said, "Mrs. McMeier, I've been walking on the water." I said, "Mr. Jesus, you're playing with fire, walking on the water." And sure enough, he got a sniffle.

MARK. A slight sniffle. Now tell me, Mrs. McMeier, is there anything else you remember about this remarkable man?

MRS. McMEIER. Well, I could go on for an eternity, of course, but I don't suppose you'd be interested in that. I do remember, however, one amusing episode, One afternoon, Mr. Jesus came to me and said, "Mrs. McMeier" he always used to address me like that, Mrs. McMeier— "I've got five thousand people coming for a picnic lunch today, can you provide me with some food?" I said, "Mr. Jesus"—I said, "five thousand people for lunch, this is bed and board for one." He said, "Well, look, do me a favor, would you?" I said, "Well look, I've only got five loaves and two fishes in the house"—he said to me—you could have knocked me down with a feather— "That is ample sufficiency." Off he went with the five loaves and two fishes, came back a few hours later with twelve basketfuls of leftovers. All I can say is, he was a very delicate carver. (*Back to* PETER *as the Shepherd and* DUDLEY *as Matthew.*)

PETER. Ahhhh . . . what a charming old lady that Mrs. McMeier. Snappy dresser . . .

DUDLEY. Yes, lovely old girl. Thank you very much indeed for your cooperation, Arthur.

PETER. Is that all you want to know about?

DUDLEY. Yes, you've given me piles.

FADE OUT

MUSIC SPOT

KWAI SONATA

(*Piano Solo*)

(DUDLEY)

FADE OUT

MINI DRAMA

VOICE. One of the strangest cases in the files of Scotland Yard is the case of the mystery mini-cab driver. Our story begins one late November evening in Hampstead. (*Sound of car stopping.* PETER *gets out of a taxi, crosses to a door* U.L. *and knocks.*)

DUDLEY. (*Behind door.*) Who's there?

PETER. Your mini cab, Lord Nesbitt.

DUDLEY. (*Enters through door.*) You're late. My car's broken down and I've got to make a speech in the House of Lords in half an hour.

PETER. Right, sir. Would you like to sit in the front or make yourself comfortable in the back?

DUDLEY. I'll sit in the back—I've got a few papers I've got to read through.

PETER. Certainly. In you get, sir. (*As* DUDLEY *gets in.*) I see yours is about seven inches long.

DUDLEY. I beg your pardon?

PETER. (*Coming around front and getting in the cab.*) I see your entry in Who's Who is about seven inches long. That's quite a length you know.

DUDLEY. Oh, I see. You—you've been reading up about me, have you?

PETER. Yes, I like to keep tabs on who I've got in the back of the car.

DUDLEY. Extraordinary hobby.

PETER. Keeps the mind alive. (*Into his handset.*) Four-five . . .

VOICE OF THE DISPATCHER. Yes, four-five.

PETER. P.O.B. Hampstead, proceeding House of Lords.

VOICE. Roger, four-five.

DUDLEY. (*As* PETER *starts the car.*) I'm due to make a speech in about half an hour's time, I'd be very obliged if you'd put your foot down.

PETER. Right. Might I suggest, at this time of night, we take a few back-doubles—it's bloody murder in the West End.

DUDLEY. Whatever you think is the quickest. (*He studies his papers.*)

VOICE. Apple-five . . . Apple-five . . . have you picked up those parcels yet? Roger, Rog, but get a move on.

PETER. How'd you get our number, sir?

DUDLEY. Oh, I think one of your chappies just dropped a card in through the letterbox. My wife gave it to me.

PETER. Oh, yes, we get a lot of customers that way —through the letterbox. (*He laughs rather menacingly.*) I said, we get a lot of customers that way. (*Laughs.*)

DUDLEY. Did I say something funny?

PETER. No sir, it's just that you have to have a laugh to stay alive in this miserable job. (*A pause.*) I wonder if we could try something, sir? A little party game that might amuse you. Knock-knock.

DUDLEY. Pardon?

PETER. It's a little game, sir. I say 'knock-knock' and you say 'who's there?'

DUDLEY. Who's there?

PETER. That's it, that's very good. Shall we try it? I think it will amuse you.

DUDLEY. (*Half-heartedly.*) Oh, yes. By all means. . . .

PETER. Knock-knock.

DUDLEY. Er—who's there?

PETER. Sam and Janet.

DUDLEY. Er—yes—that's very good. Jolly good.

PETER. No, it's not good at all, sir. I say 'Sam and Janet' and you say 'Sam and Janet who'—then I come back with the killer line. Shall we try again? Knock-knock, who's there, Sam and Janet—Sam and Janet who, from you. Then it's my line. I think the end result will tickle you.

DUDLEY. Undoubtedly.

PETER. Knock-knock.

DUDLEY. Er—who's there?

PETER. Sam and Janet.

DUDLEY. Sam—

TOGETHER. Sam and Janet Who?

PETER. (*Singing to the tune of "Some Enchanted Evening."*) Sam and Janet evening (*Laughs—sings again as* DUDLEY *seems not to comprehend.*) Sam and Janet evening—

DUDLEY. What do I say now?

PETER. You don't say anything, sir. That's it. That's the wee joke.

DUDLEY. Oh, yes, yes. That's awfully good.

VOICE. Apple-five . . . Apple-five . . . Look, how many times have I got to tell you to pick up the four brown paper parcels and dump them in a canal . . . (DUDLEY *looks up slightly surprised.*)

PETER. It must be quite nice to be in the House of Lords, you know, and make a speech now and then. Get reported in the Press—get invited on Television. It must be very nice to be famous.

DUDLEY. Well, I wouldn't say I was famous, you know.

PETER. But you're well known, aren't you, sir?

DUDLEY. Yes, yes. I'm well known, I'll grant you that.

PETER. It's all a matter of luck really, isn't it? Where you're born, who your parents were—I was found in a dust-bin in Glasgow—I never knew my parents.

DUDLEY. I'm very sorry.

VOICE. First call. Blind Beggar's Pub. Whitechapel.

PETER. (*Answering through his handset.*) Four-five.

VOICE. Second call. Blind Beggar Pub, Whitechapel.

PETER. Four-five.

VOICE. Assistance. Blind Beggar Pub!

PETER. (*Annoyed.*) Four-bloody-five here.

VOICE. Roger, four-five.

PETER. Dropping Westminster in about ten minutes. I could be in Whitechapel in twenty.

VOICE. Roger, four-five. Er—pick up torso and drop on Wimbledon Common. (DUDLEY *looks up, startled.*)

PETER. Is that cash, or account?

VOICE. Er—cash. The money's in a brown paper envelope.

PETER. Roger, Rog. (*Pause.*)

DUDLEY. Did I . . . did I hear that chap say "torso"?

PETER. Yes, that's right, sir, torso. Old Tony Torso— he's one of our regulars.

DUDLEY. God, what a bloody stupid name.

PETER. What, torso? Not really. You'd be surprised at the number of torsos floating around these days. Tony runs a very successful little Italian restaurant on the A-6.

VOICE. Apple-five . . . Apple-five. Look, it doesn't matter which canal—just dump the bloody parcels.

DUDLEY. Would you mind turning that thing off— I find it rather distracting.

PETER. What, the radiophone? By all means. (*He does.*) I've got the torso job after this—so I'm laughing. Would you mind if I put on a cassette?

DUDLEY. Whatever you like.

PETER. A little music, to while away the time as we drive through the fog. (*Very heavy Russian music is heard.* PETER *turns on the windshield wipers as he drives along in silence.*) Interesting piece, actually. Written by a young Russian—tragic life. He committed suicide at the age of thirty. He was never recognized by the critics. This music sort of reflects the despair and despondency of his life. Identify with it strongly—it conjures up a mood for me.

DUDLEY. It's bloody gloomy . . .

PETER. Yes, well, life can be very gloomy, can't it, sir? (*He takes a gun out of glove compartment.*)

DUDLEY. Good God man, what are you doing with a gun in your glove compartment?

PETER. What am I doing with a gun? I'm not doing anything with it—at the moment. But these days you never know who you're going to get in the back, eh? (*He laughs.*) That's rather good, isn't it? You never know who you'll get in the back. Do you get it, sir?

DUDLEY. No, I don't get it.

PETER. Oh, you'll get it in time—it'll come to you in a sudden blinding flash . . . (*There is a sudden blinding flash from on-coming headlights.* PETER *swerves.*)

DUDLEY. For God sake, man, look where you're going!

PETER. Bloody Nuns. Shouldn't be allowed on the road. (*Pause.*) Talking of guns, sir—which we were —didn't I read somewhere that you're on that Commission investigating the rise in violent crimes?

DUDLEY. Er, yes. Yes. I am. Why?

PETER. What do you put it down to, sir? I mean, what is it in Society that produces a Lee Harvey Oswald, a Sirhan Sirhan or that Bremer bloke who tried to gun down Wallace?

DUDLEY. Well, I think all of these chaps had **one** thing in common.

PETER. They had one thing in common, did they, sir?

DUDLEY. Yes. They were all loners.

PETER. (*After a pause.*) Loners. Take me, for example. I've no family—women have always laughed at me. I've just drifted from job to job. You could call me a loner, if you like.

DUDLEY. No (*Laughs uncomfortably.*) —you're not a loner, not in this sort of a job. I mean, you must meet lots of interesting people—take me, for example . . .

PETER. Bullshit.

DUDLEY. I wasn't suggesting . . . .

PETER. I don't like people.

DUDLEY. There's no obligation . . .

PETER. People don't like me.

DUDLEY. Of course they like you. . . . My dear chap—you're a very likeable chap. You've a marvelous sense of humor—I mean, I love that joke of yours— (*Singing.*) Sam and Janet who-o-o-

PETER. You don't really like me.

DUDLEY. I do. I know this is terribly sudden, but I'm absolutely enchanted by you . . . (*He touches* PETER *on the shoulder.*)

PETER. Don't touch me, sir. (DUDLEY *withdraws his hand quickly.*) You know my theory why people go round assassinating famous people?

DUDLEY. No, I'd be interested to hear . . .

PETER. It's their only chance in life of getting some sort of recognition.

DUDLEY. But violence will get us nowhere.

PETER. Do you not think so, sir? What about Lee Harvey Oswald? He was a nobody, a nonentity—nobody had heard of him, and then: Boom-Boom.

DUDLEY. Who's there?

DUDLEY. (*To* SIR ARTHUR.) If you would tell us something about the Frog and Peach, Sir Arthur? How did the idea come to you?

PETER. Yes, well, the idea for the Frog and Peach came to me in the bath—a great number of things come to me in the bath, mainly mosquitoes, various forms of water snakes, but on this occasion, a rather stunning and unique idea. I suddenly thought, where can a young couple go, with not too much money, feeling a bit hungry, a bit peckish, want something to eat—where can they go? Where can they go and get a really *big* frog and a damn fine peach? Where can they go? And answer came there none. And it was on this premise that I founded the Frog and Peach.

DUDLEY. On these premises?

PETER. On these precise premises, yes.

DUDLEY. How long ago did you start this venture?

PETER. Tricky to say—certainly within living memory. It was shortly after World War II. Do you remember that? Absolutely ghastly business. I was against the whole thing.

DUDLEY. I think we all were.

PETER. Yes, well, I wrote a letter.

DUDLEY. Getting back to the Frog and Peach, how has business been?

PETER. Let me answer that in two parts— Business hasn't been and there hasn't been any business. These last 35 years have been a rather lean time for us here at the old "F & P."

DUDLEY. But don't you feel that you're at a slight disadvantage being stuck out here in the middle of a bog in the heart of the Yorkshire Moors?

PETER. I think the word 'disadvantage' is awfully well chosen here. Yes, that is what we're at—we're at a disadvantage, stuck out here in the middle of a bog in the heart of the Yorkshire Moors. But I thought, rightly or wrongly—possibly both—that the people of this country were crying out for a restaurant without a parking problem. And here in the middle of a bog in the heart of the Yorkshire Moors, there is no problem parking the car. A little difficulty extricating it. But parking is sheer joy.

DUDLEY. Don't you also feel that you're at a disadvantage with regard to your menu?

PETER. Yes, this has been a terrible disadvantage to us. Have you seen it?

DUDLEY. Very briefly.

PETER. That's the only way to see it. I mean the choice is so limited. You only have two dishes to choose from. Now what are they? Blast! I should know this by heart after 35 years. Oh, yes, first there is Frog à la Pêche. Frog à la Pêche is basically a large frog, brought to your table, covered in boiling Cointreau, with a peach stuck in its mouth. It is one of the most disgusting sights I have ever seen. The only alternative to Frog à la Pêche is even worse. Pêche à la Frog. In this case, a peach is brought to your table by the waiter, again covered in boiling Cointreau—

DUDLEY. The waiter?

PETER. Very often. Very often the waiter is covered in boiling Cointreau, but the policy here is to aim the Cointreau at the peach—the peach is then sliced down the middle to reveal— Oh, God! —about 300 squiggling, black tadpoles. It is *THE* most nauseating sight I have ever seen in my life! It's enough to put you off your food—which is a damn good thing, considering what the food is like.

DUDLEY. Who does the cooking?

PETER. My wife. My wife does all the cooking, and luckily, she does all the eating as well. She's not a well woman.

DUDLEY. She's not a well woman?

PETER. She is not a well woman and she very much resents having to go down the well every morning to feed the frogs. . . . She dislikes it intensely. We have to lower her screaming on a rope. AAAAAHHHHH! Frogs don't like it either.

DUDLEY. How did you meet your wife?

PETER. I met Morag under somewhat unusual circumstances. It was during World War II—you remember that thing I tried to stop? She blew in through the window on a piece of shrapnel, became embedded in the sofa. One thing led to her mother, and we were married in the hour. Her mother is a very powerful woman. She can break a swan's wing with a blow of her nose. Kids love it at parties.

DUDLEY. Getting back to the Frog and Peach—

PETER. By all means.

DUDLEY. The whole venture of the Frog and Peach sounds a bit disastrous.

PETER. I don't think I'd use the word 'disastrous' here. I think 'catastrophic' is closer to the mark. The whole venture of the Frog and Peach has been a total failure and huge catastrophe.

DUDLEY. Do you think you've learned from your mistakes?

PETER. Oh, yes, I've learned from my mistakes and I'm sure I could repeat them exactly.

DUDLEY. Thank you, Sir Arthur Grebe-Streebling.

PETER. Strebe-Greebling.

FADE OUT

SPEECH IMPODIMENT

(DUDLEY *speaking at a desk, making an appeal.*)

DUDLEY. God ovenin. Ee window who manny owf you rollease that lits of popple on this kintry or innuble to pronince the Onglish linguage. Imogen, off you coon, the doffokulties of ovary die loaf, far sich a parson. Bat, spoch impodiments kin be carred. Ee missif, ee missif wince soffared fram sich a dofuct. Bat ifta inly throw wax of tharopoy, aikin mak missif inderstard parfektry. Mich minny is nodded for risich. Plaice guv gonerusly. Sandy notions in the frim of minny or chicks to the fillowing adrifs:

A sign appears which reads:

SPEECH IMPEDIMENT FUND
5, SMITH STREET
LONDON, W. 1 . .

(DUDLEY *says.*)
SPOCH IMPODIMENT FIND
FOVE, SMOTH STROT
LINDEN, WORST WIND

FADE OUT

TEA FOR TWO

(*A Kitchen.* DUD *is setting up a clothesline from which hangs a collection of old clothing.* PETE *enters and sits at the Kitchen table.* DUD *takes a plastic raincoat from the line and begins ironing it.*)

PETE. 'Ere, Dud, is the tea up yet?

DUD. Yeh, but I'll give it another couple of minutes to brew because we don't want to lose any of the flavor, do we?

PETE. No, we don't want to lose any of that delicious flavor bursting forth from the tea bags.

DUD. No. I'm using the larger capacity tea bags now, you know.

PETE. Oh, those bigger bags, as advertised.

DUD. Yes. They're a bit more expensive, you know, but it's worth it in the long run because when you've saved up a hundred labels you send them in to the firm and they send you back a plastic replica of a member of the Royal Family.

PETE. How delightful.

DUD. Terrific. And when you've got all 437 members of the Royal Family you send them in to the firm and they send you back a free tea bag.

PETE. A free tea bag?

DUD. Yeh. A gratis tea-bag.

PETE. What a wonderful gesture in this materialistic age.

DUD. Well, it gives you a ray of hope, doesn't it?

PETE. It certainly does, yeh. Well, while you were making the tea I was reading an interesting article about the emancipation of women by Ms. Germaine Greer. (*He shows* DUDLEY *a magazine.*)

DUD. Oh, yeh?

PETE. Did you peruse the item aforesaid?

DUD. Well I got about half way through the first word and then I had to nip off and check on my rice pudding, cause my pinger was going.

PETE. Well it was rather an interesting article about the subjugation of women throughout the ages—you know, how they've been held down and dominated by the male.

DUD. Oh, yeh?

PETE. (*Pointing to the tea which* DUDLEY *is about to pour.*) You be mum, will you, please?

DUD. Yes, certainly. (*He pours.*)

PETE. Not too much milk. You made it a bit wishy-washy last time.

DUD. Sorry.

PETE. And I think Miss Greer, who is not an unintelligent woman—

DUD. No, let's give her that.

PETE. Let's give her that—has raised a number of interesting and salient points.

DUD. (*Looking at the magazine.*) Yeh . . . she raised two on the cover that caught my attention.

PETE. Don't follow you. There's nothing written on the cover.

DUD. No, the points I was referring to were not of a literary nature. They had a certain visual appeal.

PETE. You are referring to her tits?

DUD. Her T.I.T.S.—yes.

PETE. Do you realize you are doing precisely what Miss Greer objects to—namely you are treating women purely as sexual objects.

DUD. I wouldn't mind it the other way round . . .

PETE. What?

DUD. I wouldn't mind having ladies use me as a sexual object—having them satiate their lust upon my body.

PETE. But surely you'd rather be respected for your mind than your body.

DUD. No. Well, eventually, yes, but I'd like them to give my body a good going over first.

PETE. Oh, so you'd like them to start on your body

and then gradually work their way down towards your mind.

DUD. Yeh . . . yeh . . . that sounds all right.

PETE. Are those scones ready yet?

DUD. (*Looking in the oven.*) Yeh, they should be done now.

PETE. They should be, they've been in there for three days.

DUD. Well if you want something nice, you have to wait for it. (*He brings the scones over to the table.*) I think that whatever Miss Greer says, the lot of women has improved since Victorian times, you know.

PETE. For a lot of women.

DUD. I mean, in Victorian times a woman's life was pure drudgery.

PETE. Mind you, there are still countries in the world today where the woman is completely dominated by the male.

DUD. Oh, really. Where?

PETE. Well, take the Far East, for example. Would you butter this scone? (DUDLEY *starts to butter the scone with a huge piece of butter.*) There, in the Far East, the woman is treated as a mere beast of burden. (*Referring to* DUDLEY'S *work on the scone.*) No, not too thick.

DUD. (*Referring to the scone.*) Oh, sorry. (*He reduces the butter on the scone.*) Is that O.K.?

PETE. Yeh.

DUD. Do you want it all around the edges?

PETE. Of course I do, I'm not going to start in the middle, am I?

DUD. Is that O.K.?

PETE. It'll do. You see, in the Far East, the woman is treated as a mere beast of burden. Do you know the woman has to walk ten yards behind the husband.

DUD. Yeh?

PETE. The only time she is allowed to walk in front of her husband is in suspected mine fields.

DUD. Good Lord. That's terrible.

PETE. (PETER *drinks some tea*.) So is this tea.

DUD. *What?*

PETE. This tea is terrible. You smell it.

DUD. (DUDLEY *smells the tea in the pot and reacts with disgust*.) Oh, bloody hell!

PETE. (*Smelling his cup of tea*.) Like the Ganges in here!

DUD. (*Inspecting the contents of the pot*.) Oh, look. I've got Princess Anne up the spout. I've never seen her like that before. I'll just throw in a couple of tea bags and drown her out. (*He goes to drawer to get some teabags*.) It's interesting what you were saying about Man's basic hostility to women because I think that God, with His usual perspicacity, has made Man the aggressor in the eternal war of the sexes. I mean, since Primordial times, when Diana Dors ruled the Earth, Man has been the hunter. Where did I put those bloody tea bags?

PETE. You usually secrete them in that box by the stove.

DUD. (*Finding some teabags*.) Getting back to what Miss Greer says, I think she overstates her case.

PETE. She blows things out of all proportion.

DUD. . . . There are so many things that ladies have that we men could never share in. I mean . . . not for us, the exquisite pleasure of a baby suckling at our breast. (*He is preparing* PETE's *tea again*.) Milk and two lumps, as usual?

PETE. Er . . . thank you, yes. I agree. Man, denied this ultimate ecstasy, is forced to channel his mind into the realms of Art and Science.

DUD. Yeh, he's bound to.

PETE. And if you look back through the anals (sic) of history, where will you find a female equivalent of say, Ludwig von Beethoven?

DUD. Yeh, Beethoven and his incomparable Symphonies.

PETE. Schopenhauer.

DUD. Schopenhauer and his lyrical Nocturnes.

PETE. Of course, I think you have to go along with Professor Shockley here and face the fact that the whole thing is tied up in our Genes. The Genetic Factor. But these Women's Libbers will not accept it. Do you know, they regard the brassiere as a symbol of masculine enslavement?

DUD. Oh, but that's ridiculous isn't it?

PETE. Yeh.

DUD. We didn't push them into their brassieres, did we?

PETE. No, we did not.

DUD. I ask you, did we males force the females into their brassieres?

PETE. No.

DUD. I've been trying for years to get them out of them.

PETE. And who was it that invented the brassiere? For the benefit of ladies.

DUD. Who?

PETE. A man.

DUD. Might have known.

PETE. Dr. Otto Titsling, working away in his laboratory in Hamburg, first came up with "der busten unter halter gesellschaft." And look at all the other things that men have been coming up with for ladies . . .

DUD. Oh, yeh.

PETE. Throughout the centuries. The list is enormous. The kitchen stove.

DUD. A miracle.

PETE. The ironing board.

DUD. And of course, in recent years, the paper pantie.

PETE. An enormous breakthrough.

DUD. Man, you see, has invented the paper pantie especially for ladies. They're so economical. Whereas in the past, Mrs. Woolley used to have to toil for hours over her knickers in the sink, now all she has to do of an evening is go over them with an eraser.

PETE. Dropping Mrs. Woolley's knickers for the moment, I think we have to face the fact that thanks to the Pill, another man-made device for the benefit of ladies of the opposite sex, women are becoming, increasingly, the sexual aggressors.

DUD. Oh, they're bound to.

PETE. I don't know if you're familiar with *Cosmopolitan*.

DUD. What's that?

PETE. It's a ladies periodical that comes out monthly.

DUD. Ah . . . no . . . don't know it.

PETE. You don't know that one?

DUD. No.

PETE. Well, in that magazine, all the stress is laid on the onus of the male . . .

DUD. Ooooh . . .

PETE. . . . to satisfy the female, sexually speaking.

DUD. Oh, yeh—all that stuff about how it takes longer for the female to feel . . . dirty . . .

PETE. Not quite the scientific term, but how it takes a lady a little longer to become sexually aroused.

Dud. Yeh . . . it's all that stuff about eroneous zones, isn't it?

Pete. No . . . no, it's not eroneous, it's erogenous. Eroneous is where you go wrong.

Dud. That's where I go wrong.

Pete. Oh, you go wrong on the erogenous zones?

Dud. Yeh.

Pete. Yeh, well I'm not surprised, there's so many of the bleeding things.

Dud. Well, a lady's peppered from head to foot with erogenous zones.

Pete. (*Pointing to his magazine.*) Have you seen these diagrams?

Dud. Of the erogenous zones?

Pete. Yeah.

Dud. I daren't look . . .

Pete. It's like a map of the Underground.

Dud. A man is hard put to know where to start his sexual voyage.

Pete. Yeh, well not the Northern Line.

Dud. Yeh. I mean, what may attract one lady, may repel the other.

Pete. This is the dilemma.

Dud. This is the eternal dilemma. You could spend six hours tickling her calves with a Japanese feather device, as advertised, when all she needs to get her going is your hot breath on her . . . on her . . . (*Embarrassed.*) do-dahs . . . her busty substances.

Pete. On her busty substances.

Pete. I think, ladies, having all these many and various erogenous zones about their person—I think the least they could do is to label them.

Dud. Yeh.

PETE. You know, label them in order of preference.

DUD. Yeh.

PETE. Then at least you could be certain of starting off on the right foot.

DUD. That's a daft place to start . . .

PETE. I was speaking metaphorically, I wasn't suggesting you go crawling round the floor at parties sucking ladies' toes.

DUD. Oh.

PETE. Though, of course, that might turn them on in these freaky, degenerate days we live in. 'Have a go —suck a toe!' That might be the new slogan for the Salacious Seventies.

DUD. Yeh, count me out.

PETE. Count me out. Anyway, I'm off to the Pub for a pint of beer. Are you coming?

DUD. Yeah.

PETE. Might meet a few girls down there.

DUD. Oh, I'd better take the diagram then. (*Reaches for magazine as they exit.*)

FADE OUT

(*Song*)

GOODBYE

by DUDLEY MOORE

Now is the time to say good-bye,
Now is the time to yield a sigh,
Now is the time to wend our way,
Until we meet again some sunny day.

Good-bye, good-bye, we're leaving you,
Skiddlee-dah. Good-bye.
We wish a fond good-bye,
Fa-ta-ta-ta faddle-a-ta.
Good-bye, good-bye, we're leaving you,
Skiddlee-dah. Goodbye
We wish a fond good-bye,
Fa-ta ta-ta ta. La, da,
Da, la, da-da, la la da da da,
Ra da da da da da da, good-bye,
Good-bye, we're leaving you—
Skiddlee-dah. Good-bye,
We wish a fond good-bye.

CURTAIN

The Gingerbread Lady

NEIL SIMON
(Little Theatre) Comedy-Drama
3 Men, 3 Women—Interior

Maureen Stapleton played the Broadway part of a popular singer who has gone to pot with booze and sex. We meet her at the end of a ten-week drying out period at a sanitarium, when her friend, her daughter, and an actor try to help her adjust to sobriety. But all three have the opposite effect on her. The friend is so constantly vain she loses her husband; the actor, a homosexual, is also doomed, and indeed loses his part three days before an opening; and the daughter needs more affection than she can spare her mother. Enter also a former lover louse, who ends up giving her a black eye. The birthday party washes out, the gingerbread lady falls off the wagon and careens onward to her own tragic end.

> "He has combined an amusing comedy with the atmosphere of great sadness. His characteristic wit and humor are at their brilliant best, and his serious story of lost misfits can often be genuinely and deeply touching."—N.Y. Post. "Contains some of the brightest dialogue Simon has yet composed."—N.Y. Daily News. "Mr. Simon's play is as funny as ever—the customary avalanche of hilarity, and landslide of pure unbuttoned joy . . . Mr. Simon is a funny, funny man—with tears running down his cheek."—N.Y. Times.

The Sunshine Boys

NEIL SIMON
(All Groups) Comedy
5 Men, 2 Women

An ex-vaudeville team, Al Lewis and Willie Clarke, in spite of playing together for forty-three years, have a natural antipathy for one another. (Willie resents Al's habit of poking a finger in his chest, or perhaps accidentally spitting in his face). It has been eleven years since they have performed together, when along comes CBS-TV, who is preparing a "History of Comedy" special, that will of course include Willie and Al—the "Lewis and Clark" team back together again. In the meantime, Willie has been doing spot commercials, like for Schick (the razor blade shakes) or for Frito-Lay potato chips (he forgets the name), while Al is happily retired. The team gets back together again, only to have Al poke his finger in Willie's chest, and accidentally spit in his face.

> ". . . the most delightful play Mr. Simon has written for several seasons and proves why he is the ablest current author of stage humor."—Watts, N. Y. Post. "None of Simon's comedies has been more intimately written out of love and a bone-deep affinity with the theatrical scene and temperament." Time. ". . . another hit for Neil Simon in this shrewdly balanced, splendidly performed and rather touching slice of the show-biz life."—Watt, New York Daily News. "(Simon) . . . writes the most dependably crisp and funny dialogue around . . . always well-set and polished to a high lustre."—WABC-TV. ". . . a vaudeville act within a vaudeville act . . . Simon has done it again."—WCBS-TV.

CEMENTVILLE
by Jane Martin
Comedy
Little Theatre

(5m., 9f.) Int. The comic sensation of the 1991 Humana Festival at the famed Actors Theatre of Louisville, this wildly funny new play by the mysterious author of *Talking With* and *Vital Signs* is a brilliant portrayal of America's fascination with fantasy entertainment, "the growth industry of the 90's." We are in a run-down locker room in a seedy sports arena in the Armpit of the Universe, "Cementville, Tennessee," with the scurviest bunch of professional wrasslers you ever saw. This is decidedly a small-time operation—not the big time you see on TV. The promoter, Bigman, also appears in the show. He and his brother Eddie are the only men, though; for the main attraction(s) are the "ladies." There's Tiger, who comes with a big drinking problem and a small dog; Dani, who comes with a large chip on her shoulder against Bigman, who owes all the girls several weeks' pay; Lessa, an ex-Olympic shotputter with delusions that she is actually employed presently in athletics; and Netty, an overweight older woman who appears in the ring dressed in baggy pajamas, with her hair in curlers, as the character "Pajama Mama." There is the eager-beaver go-fer Nola, a teenager who dreams of someday entering the glamorous world of pro wrestling herself. And then, there are the Knockout Sisters, refugees from the Big Time but banned from it for heavy-duty abuse of pharmaceuticals as well as having gotten arrested *in flagrante delicto* with the Mayor of Los Angeles. They have just gotten out of the slammer; but their indefatigable manager, Mother Crocker ("Of the Auto-Repair Crockers") hopes to get them reinstated, if she can keep them off the white powder. Bigman has hired the Knockout Sisters as tonight's main attraction, and the fur really flies along with the sparks when the other women find out about the Knockout Sisters. Bigman has really got his hands full tonight. He's gotta get the girls to tear each other up in the ring, not the locker room; he's gotta deal with tough-as-nails Mother Crocker; he's gotta keep an arena full of tanked-up rubes from tearing up the joint—and he's gotta solve the mystery of who bit off his brother Eddie's dick last night.   (#5580)

New Comedies from
Samuel French, Inc.

THE LADY IN QUESTION (Little Theatre.-Comedy)
by Charles Busch.
5m., 4f. 1 int., 1 ext. w/insert.

This hilarious spoof of every trashy damsel-in-distress-vs.-the Nazis movie you ever saw
packed them in Off Broadway, where the irrepressible Mr. Busch starred as Gertrude
Garnet, world-renowned concert pianist and world-class hedonist. On tour in Bavaria,
Gertrude finds her Nazi hosts charming; until, that is, she unwittingly becomes
enlisted in a plot by Prof Erik Maxwell to free his mother, a famous actress who has
appeared in an anti-Nazi play, from the clutches of the Fuhrer's fearsome minions. At
first, Gertrude is more concerned about the whereabouts of her missing cosmetics
bag; but when her best friend and travelling companion Kitty is murdered by the Nazi
swine, Gertrude agrees to help Erik by manipulating the Nazi Baron Von Elsner,
whose mansion becomes the escape route. Of course, Gertrude and Erik fall in love;
and, of course, there is a desperate dash (on *skis*, no less!) to the safety of the Swiss
border, where Gertrude and Erik find True Love. Mr. Busch's send-up of this film
genre is so witty and well-constructed that, as the NY Times pointed out, it would be
just as entertaining if the role of Gertrude were played by a woman. "Bewitchingly
entertaining. I couldn't have had a better time, unless perhaps someone had given me
popcorn."—N.Y. Post. "Hilarious."—N.Y. Times.
(#14182)

RED SCARE ON SUNSET (Advanced Groups-Comedy)
by Charles Busch.
5m., 3f. Unit set.

This Off-Broadway hit is set in 1950's Hollywood during the blacklist days. This is a
hilarious comedy that touches on serious subjects by the author of *Vampire Lesbians
of Sodom*. Mary Dale is a musical comedy star who discovers to her horror that her
husband, her best friend, her director and houseboy are all mixed up in a communist
plot to take over the movie industry. Among their goals is the dissolution of the star
system! Mary's conversion from Rodeo Drive robot to McCarthy marauder who
ultimately names names including her husband's makes for outrageous, thought
provoking comedy. The climax is a wild dream sequence where Mary imagines she's
Lady Godiva, the role in the musical she's currently filming. Both right and left are
skewered in this comic melodrama. "You have to champion the ingenuity of Busch's
writing which twirls twist upon twist and spins into comedy heaven."—Newsday.
(#19982)

More Children's Plays
from Samuel French, Inc.

BRIDGE TO TERABITHIA (All Groups.) Children's Play with music. Katherine Paterson and Stephanie S. Tolan. Music by Steve Liebman. 3m., 6f., plus extras. Unit set. This powerful adaptation, supported by a lyrical score, focuses the humor, warmth and emotional intensity of Katherine Paterson's Newbery Award-winning novel to create a stage work of dramatic impact. Jesse Aarons, alienated from the pragmatism of family and rural Virginia culture, draws and dreams of becoming something special, but for now "the fastest runner in the fifth grade." Leslie Burke, the new girl from the city and ultimate outsider, first beats him at running, then opens for him a larger world of the imagination, of art and literature. Together they create Terabithia, a fantasy kingdom where they are safe from those who don't understand them, and where their friendship grows as Jesse's world expands. When tragedy strikes, it is the strength he has gained in Terabithia that takes Jesse forward on his own and lets him share the magic and the dreams.   (#4200)

THE LAST CARNIVAL (Little Theatre.) Ecological comedy with music. Stephen M. Press. Over 15 characters (may be played by 6 actors). Unit set. A kid comes to a carnival But this carnival is different. This carnival is the earth. Running everything is Carny who only cares about having fun and putting on a good show! Among the carnival performers are Paul Bunyan, Buffalo Bill, John Henry, Robert Fulton and Dr. Schlemiel Faustus who will sell you anything—from the Big Bomb to a cure for dandruff or cancer! At The Last Carnival you'll visit the Tunnel of Love which is in a sewer, mow down endangered species at The Shooting Gallery and lose the Redwood Forests at the Wheel of Fortune! The other characters everybody knows—the speedway Devil Driver, the rock stars of the Rotten Roll Band, Filthy Flora whose ecdysiast act will surprise you, and the one who knows all, Miriam the Mentalist. All perform and pollute the earth. But it's all done with crazy comedy and famous music. After all, who cares about tomorrow!? Ask the kid. "Haunting, magical, timeless, darkly humorous and entertaining ... As you enter the strange world of this play, be prepared to be hustled, amused, shocked and enlightened."—Taconic Newsp.   (#14600)

Other Publications for Your Interest

CINDERELLA WALTZ
(ALL GROUPS—COMEDY)
By DON NIGRO

4 men, 5 women—1 set

Rosey Snow is trapped in a fairy tale world that is by turns funny and a little frightening, with her stepsisters Goneril and Regan, her demented stepmother, her lecherous father, a bewildered Prince, a fairy godmother who sings salty old sailor songs, a troll and a possibly homicidal village idiot. A play which investigates the archetypal origins of the world's most popular fairy tale and the tension between the more familiar and charming Perrault version and the darker, more ancient and disturbing tale recorded by the brothers Grimm. Grotesque farce and romantic fantasy blend in a fairy tale for adults.

(#5208)

ROBIN HOOD
(LITTLE THEATRE—COMEDY)
By DON NIGRO

14 men, 8 women—(more if desired.) Unit set.

In a land where the rich get richer, the poor are starving, and Prince John wants to cut down Sherwood Forest to put up an arms manufactory, a slaughterhouse and a tennis court for the well to do, this bawdy epic unites elements of wild farce and ancient popular mythologies with an environmentalist assault on the arrogance of wealth and power in the face of poverty and hunger. Amid feeble and insane jesters, a demonic snake oil salesman, a corrupt and lascivious court, a singer of eerie ballads, a gluttonous lusty friar and a world of vivid and grotesque characters out of a Brueghel painting, Maid Marian loses her clothes and her illusions among the poor and Robin tries to avoid murder and elude the Dark Monk of the Wood who is Death and also perhaps something more.

(#20075)